Lucas and His Loco Beans

Story by Ramona Moreno Winner
Illustrations by Nicole Velasquez
Flip Book by Mary McConnell

A  **BrainSTORM 3000**
Publication
www.brainstorm3000.com

Printed in Hong Kong by Toppan Printing Co.

abrazo
hug

Abuelo, Abuelo, I
yelled as I ran

I hugged him and
held him, grabbed
hold of his hand.

abuelo
grandfather

grito
yell

Each *verano* I
visit *abuelo's*
small ranch.

We fish and we
swim when given
a chance.

Early one morning
we walked a long
ways.

Over rocks and
through *ramas* we
trekked through
the maze.

ramas
branches

ranchito
ranch

verano
summer

lugar
place

montañas
mountains

Where are we going *abuelo*? I asked.

To a *lugar* in the mountains where I played in the past.

I was tired and wanted to get there real soon.

My *panza* was rumbling as it approached noon.

panza
stomach

As we reached some tall *matas* with shiny green leaves.

My *Abuelo* said: *Éstos son* the right trees!

Dame tu mano and slowly come near.

Keep very still. Now what do you hear?

dame tu mano
give me your hand

éstos son
these are

matas
plants

abajo
down

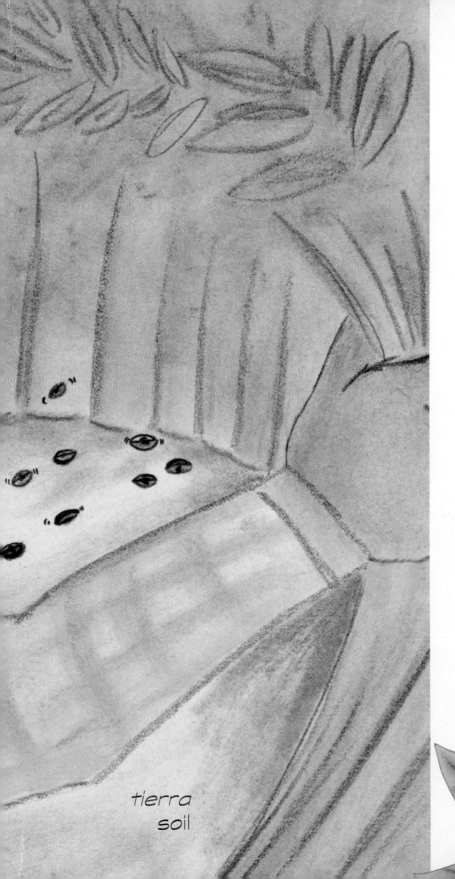

He pushed apart
bushes and then
pointed down.

Many *semillas*
were jumping
around.

Click, click, click,
click, snap, snap,
snap.

The soil looked
alive, and I quickly
stepped back.

semillas
seeds

tierra
soil

¿*Qué son*? I asked as I dropped to my knees.

Son brincadores or Mexican Jumping Beans.

Are they alive? I asked quite surprised.

Sí, i'll tell you a *cuento* if you sit by my side.

¿qué son?
what are they?

cuento
story

sí
yes

son
they are

hoy
today

joven
young

When I was *joven* as you are today.

I carried some with me in a *caja* to play.

The worm wiggles around for most of the day.

Eating the inside of the *semilla* away.

caja
box

After several
meses they'd go
very still,

Abandoned *solos*
on an old windowsill.

I would forget
them—until one
spring day,

The *polillas* would
leave the seed,
and all fly away.

meses
months

polillas
moths

solos
alone

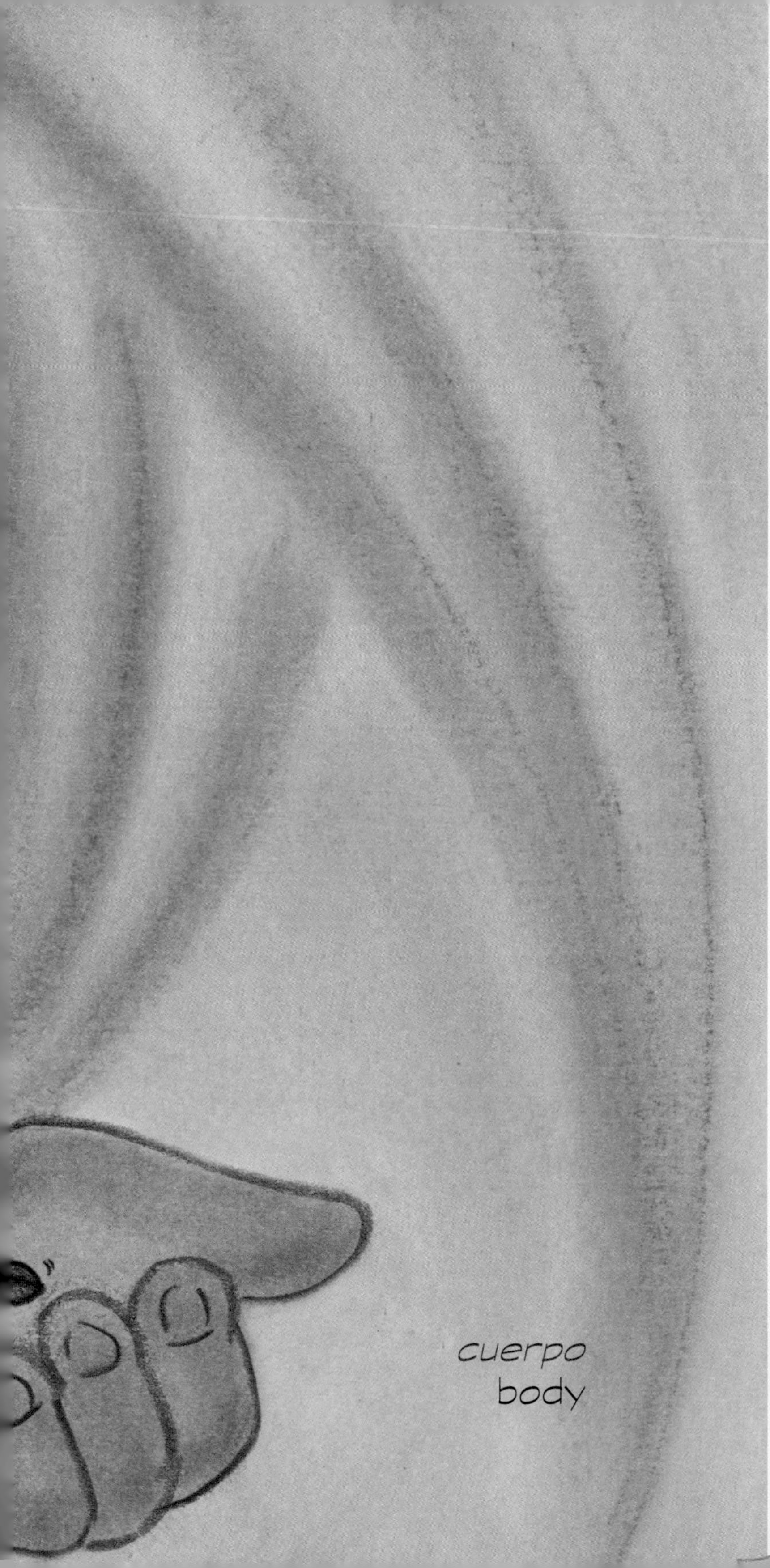

Lucas—take
some beans in
your *mano* and
you'll see.

Your warm body
los hace mover
like crazy.

The loco beans
were snapping and
clicking in my hand.

They wiggled and
moved and I thought:
OH MAN!

los hace mover
makes them move

cuerpo
body

Abuelo, will these beans grow at home? I asked.

To share them with *amigos* would be quite a blast!

Here—the weather is perfect for jumping beans to grow.

If they grow in *otros lugares*, I really don't know.

otros lugares
other places

amigos
friends

tiempo
weather

We got back *muy tarde*, the moon lighting our way.

I was dusty y thirsty but I had a great day.

muy tarde
very late

luna
moon

y
and

I love *mi Abuelo*; I look forward to school.

Sharing these jumping beans will be really COOL!

yo
I

escuela
school

mi
my

compartir
share

Facts in English

A jumping bean is not a bean. It is a small, thin-shelled section of a seed capsule containing the larva (worm) of a small gray moth (Laspeyresia saltitans).

See Diagram one.

Early summer, the female moth lays her eggs on the green, immature capsules of the female flower.

See Diagram two.

In the early summer, a single seed splits into three sections. Each section can contain a moth's larva.

See Diagram three.

It is not good for the plant to have worms in all the seeds. If this were to occur there would be no seeds to be carried away by birds and replanted.

Once in the seed, the larva spins silk to line the inside of its new home.

See Diagram four.

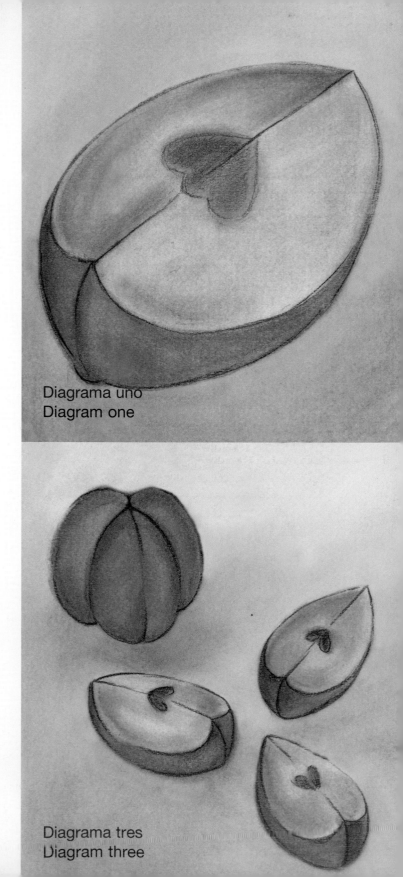

Diagrama uno
Diagram one

Diagrama tres
Diagram three

Datos en español

El brincador no es un frijol. Es una sección de la cáscara de una semilla que contiene la larva (gusano) de una pequeña polilla gris (Laspeyresia saltitans).
Ver Diagrama uno.

A principios del verano, la polilla hembra pone sus huevos en las cápsulas verdes e inmaduras de la flor femenina.
Ver Diagrama dos.

Al empezar el verano, la semilla se divide en tres secciones. Cada una de ellas puede contener la larva de una polilla.
Ver Diagrama tres.

No es beneficioso para la planta tener gusanos en cada semilla. De otro modo, no hay semillas que los pájaros puedan llevarse para ser replantadas.

En cuanto entra a la semilla, la larva teje el hilo de seda que cubre el interior de su nueva casa.
Ver Diagrama cuatro.

Diagrama dos
Diagram two

Diagrama cuatro
Diagram four

Facts in English

The larva grasps the silken lining with its forelegs and by snapping its body, it is able to strike the seed wall and make the seed roll and move about.

See Diagram five.

The larva moves around to access eatable parts of the seed and to reach shade.

As winter approaches, the larva is ready to wrap itself in silk for its pupa stage (this is the final stage it undergoes before becoming a moth). Before it can do this, it must precut an exit door so that it can exit as a moth.

See Diagram six.

Early summer the pupa transforms into a moth and emerges using the precut exit door it prepared several months earlier when it was a larva.

See Diagram seven.

The moths then find mates and the whole cycle begins once again. If there are no jumping bean shrubs around, the moths will die. That is why the jumping beans can be sent all over the world. They cannot infest any other type of bush or tree.

See Diagram eight.

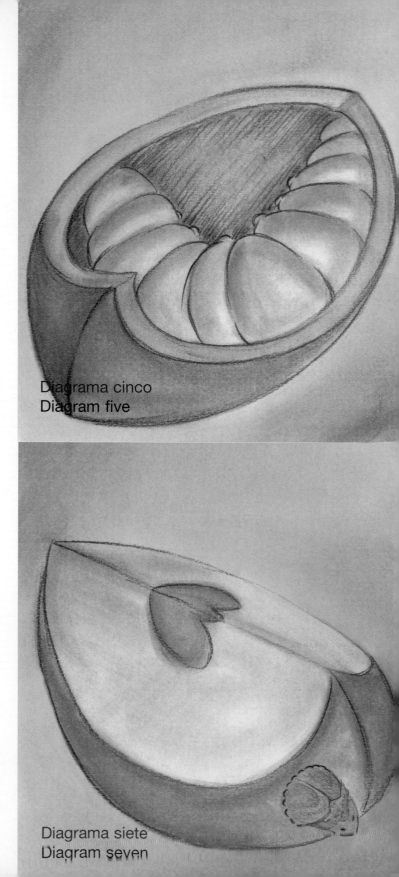

Diagrama cinco
Diagram five

Diagrama siete
Diagram seven

Datos en español

La larva coge el hilo de seda con sus patas delanteras y al mover su cuerpo rápidamente, golpea el interior de la semilla, haciendo que ésta ruede.

Ver Diagrama cinco.

La larva se mueve para comerse lo adentro de la semilla y hallar sombra.

Cuando se acerca el invierno, la larva está lista para envolverse en seda y pasar al estado de crisálida (ésta es la última etapa de su transformación). Antes debe cortar un orificio que le permita salir de la semilla siendo polilla.

Ver Diagrama seis.

Al llegar el verano, se transforma en una polilla y se sale por el orificio que hizo meses atrás cuando todavía era una larva.

Ver Diagrama siete.

Las polillas encuentran compañeros y el ciclo comienza una vez más. Si no hay arbustos de brincadores en el lugar, las polillas se mueren. Es por eso que los brincadores pueden enviarse a todo el mundo. No pueden infestar otra planta o árbol.

Ver Diagrama ocho.

Diagrama seis
Diagram six

Diagrama ocho
Diagram eight

Choose the correct meaning for each word.

1. Abuelo (ah BWEL oh)   a) grandma   b) grandpa

2. Grito (GREE toe)   a) boat   b) yell

3. Ramas (RRAH mahs)   a) branches   b) goats

4. Verano (beh RAH noe)   a) summer   b) spring

5. Ranchito (rran CHEE toe)   a) ranch   b) room

6. Lugar (loo GAR)   a) look   b) place

7. Montañas (moan THAH nee oz)   a) music   b) mountains

8. Panza (PAHN sah)   a) paws   b) stomach

9. Éstos (EHS toes)   a) these   b) sticks

10. Dame (THAH meh)   a) give me   b) dime

11. Matas (MAH thahs)   a) mats   b) plants

12. Abajo (ah BAH hoe)   a) banjo   b) down

13. Tierra (THEE ehrr ah)   a) soil   b) crown

14. Semillas (seh MEE yahs)   a) seeds   b) soap

15. Sí (SEE)   a) look   b) yes

16. Cuento (KOOEHN thoe)   a) count   b) story

17. Que (keh)   a) what   b) where

18. Son (soen)   a) boy   b) are

19. Hoy (ohy)   a) hello   b) today

20. Joven (HOE ben)   a) happy   b) young

21. Caja (KAH ha)   a) come   b) box

22. Meses (mehs es)   a) months   b) mess

23. Polillas (poe LEE yahs)   a) moths   b) beans

24. Solos (SOE lohs)   a) alone   b) sun

25. Amigos (ah MEE goes)   a) ants   b) friends

26. Tiempo (tee M poe)   a) beat   b) weather

27. Otro (OH throe)   a) our   b) other

28. Mano (MAH noe)   a) hand   b) brother

29. Cuerpo (KWHER poe)   a) body   b) heavy

30. Mover (moe BEHR)   a) mow   b) move

31. Tu (thoo)   a) two   b) your

32. Escuela (es KWHE lah)   a) school   b) ladder

33. Abrazo (ah BRA soe)   a) hug   b) get

34. Yo (yoh)   a) me   b) you

35. Mi (mee)   a) my   b) your

36. Y (ee)   a) and   b) yes

37. Tarde (THAR deh)   a) long   b) late

Answer Key

Ramona and Lucas Winner

Why Lucas and His Jumping Beans?

While shopping, I was attracted to this basket filled with small plastic containers that were emitting noticeable clicking sounds. I looked closer and found them to be Mexican jumping beans. I bought a little container and took them home to my son, Lucas. He was so fascinated by the jumping beans that we decided to check out the website listed on the bottom of the box. We learned so much fun stuff that I decided to write a story about them. Lucas never had the chance to know his own abuelo, but I fondly remember how he would share his wisdom about the desert with me as a child. If he were alive today, he would have found great pleasure in sharing jumping beans with Lucas.

For more books by Ramona and further information please visit www.brainstorm3000.com
To purchase the Mexican Jumping Beans go to www.u-payless.com or www.jbean.com